HELLO MY NAME IS
Amineko

Creative Publishing international

First published in the United States of America in 2010 by
Creative Publishing international, Inc., a member of
Quayside Publishing Group
400 First Avenue North
Suite 300
Minneapolis, MN 55401
1-800-328-3895
www.creativepub.com
Visit www.Craftside.Typepad.com for a behind-the-scenes peek at our crafty world!

Originally published in Japanese language by SHUFU TO SEIKATSU SHA
English language translation & production by World Book Media, LLC, info@worldbookmedia.com
English translation rights arranged with SHUFU TO SEIKATSU SHA, Tokyo
Through Timo Associates, Inc., Tokyo

ISBN-13: 978-1-58923-571-7
ISBN-10: 1-58923-571-1

10 9 8 7 6 5 4 3 2 1

Printed in China

HELLO MY NAME IS

Amineko

The Story of a Crafty Crochet Cat

Make me and all my stuff too!

Nekoyama

Creative Publishing
international

INTRODUCTION

The crocheted cats inside this book are a special breed. When I first made one, I had no idea what was about to happen. One day, I decided that I wanted to try and crochet a little cat that appeared to be asleep. It would need a sleepy expression on its face, flexible legs and a flexible tail to curl up in all sorts of ways for the perfect cat nap. Cats seem to sleep anywhere and have a knack for wedging themselves into the strangest spots. With all this in mind I began my crochet project and what resulted was a little cat that seemed to have a big personality—meet Amineko!

Each crocheted Amineko will be a little different—no two are ever identical. It is amazing how one basic design can be altered in small ways to create a breadth of appearance and personality. Choosing different yarn weights, yarn colors, and facial expressions will contribute to each cat's unique look. Before I knew it, I had an entire Amineko family in my house, and you can too. Don't forget to name them and play with them—they love to pose for pictures! I hope you are as inspired as I have been by these whimsical new friends. This book is about having fun.

Enjoy!

In Japanese "ami" means crochet and "neko" means cat

CONTENTS

PART 1:
ALL ABOUT AMINEKO

Good Morning Amineko!

Green Tea

Amineko is hard to wake up...

Green tea helps...

...but your Amineko may be finicky...

...and want juice instead.

Snooping Amineko

My, oh my, this is good stuff.

Hey, that part is about me...

Well that's a rather catty remark!

AMINEKO STOP READING MY DIARY!
Meeooww!

Sweeping Up

I'm on sweeping duty.

Me too.

Me three!

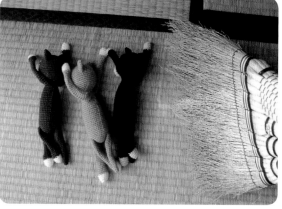

We love sweeping!

Perception

Glasses make you look smart.

They don't feel so smart down here.

Now I feel smart, but really dizzy.

I'll just keep them up here for now. Whew!

PLAY TIME

Curiosity Killed the Cat

Hmmm... what's this?

Bonk! "Ouch!"

It's a futon beater.

Good thing I have nine lives...

A Game of Cat & Mouse

This is a funny looking mouse.

Let's play!

Stop working and play with me!

AMINEKO DON'T YOU DARE!
With Amineko in the house, remember to save documents frequently!

Rubber Band Ring Toss

Hide & Sleep

Ok guys, I'm going to try and hook your ears.

This game is a variation on "hide and seek."

Don't move!

OK my eyes are closed.

We don't want to play anymore.

Mine too!

Fine. I'm going to take a nap.

Zzzz...
Game over.

Wanderlust

What are you doing?

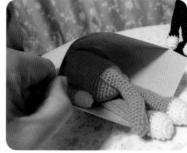

Are you putting yourself inside an envelope?

Bon Voyage!

Telephone Troubles

What?!

Why are these things so complicated?

I can't hear you!

Hmmm, I wonder what those little holes are for?

Lost in Translation

Sharing

Amineko, where are you?

Amineko patiently waits for his friend to join him.

What are you doing?

Food tastes so much better when you share it.

Aha! Lost in another Manga book (sigh).

Hey Amineko, you have a seed on your nose!

EVERYTHING IS A TOY

The Box

Cats love boxes...

...the smaller the better...

...even this box.

Cat-a-strophic!

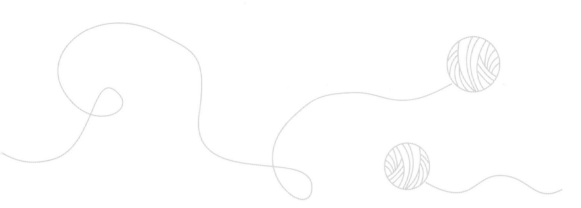

Magic Yarn

And now for my amazing body-stretching trick!

I will crawl into this ball of yarn and become longer.

Here I go.

Ta-da!

Close Call

Boy that sure is sticky.

Get it off me!

I'm all tangled up! Help!

Are you OK?

Thanks guys, I thought I was going to die.

Stinky Shoes

Sniff. Sniff.

Once again, curiosity killed the cat.

I don't feel so good...

BIG EATER

Accounting Blues

Missing Green

$4.95 + $16.22 + $3.47...

Have you guys seen Green?

We're over our food budget this month.

Seen Green lately?

OK, no extras, like those chicken treats or cat nip...

Seen Green around?

I can still dream!

Wake me up at snack time... Zzzzz.

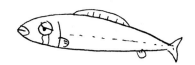

Nice Aromas

I *love* the way this pot smells!

Seven hours later...

I've got to get a grip...

Art Class

Let's look at our drawings.

This one looks like shish kebab.

Green, all you draw is food. I'm a starving artist!

Miso Soup

I'm a cat and I need protein!

Voilà!

Ummm, it's kind of small, don't you think?

The Cake

I thought I put that cake in the fridge...

...I see small black ears.

BURP!

Inside the Cream Puff

Well, at least I have this cream puff.

Suspicious...

...very suspicious...

Cat got your tongue?

My Favorite Food

I love shellfish!

But not water.

It pays to be brave.

SEIZA: seiza is the term for the traditional sitting posture in Japan

Amineko demonstrates:

Step 1: Bend from knees.

Step 2: Rest hind-quarters on heels.

Overhead View
Should I take a chicken treat...

Front View
...or some cat nip?

Back View
Amineko looks so peaceful, he must be in a deep meditation!

Side View
Can I have my treat now?

SLOUCHING SEIZA

2 minutes—Straight and tall

4 minutes—Slowly bending forward

6 minutes—Leg are placed out straight.

8 minutes—Phew!

10 minutes—This is duck posture, the formal sitting style of Amineko.

Purrrfect Postures for Amineko

Pose #1— "Chillin' on a bench"

Pose #2—"Confused Kitty"

Pose #4—"Pretzel"

Pose #3—"Watching the bird feeder"

Begin by crossing arms then pull tight!

Here we have combined variations on "Watching the bird feeder" and "Pretzel."

Sitting on your friend is *not* a pose.

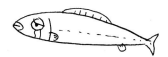

Vegetarian

I don't like sardines or squid.

Actually, I'm a vegetarian.

I love edamame.

Hmm, I could put them into my pocket when no one is watching...

...but what if somebody sees, how embarrassing...(sweating)

45 minutes later, his legs now asleep...

"Amineko, didn't you like your dinner?" Uh, well, do you have any edamame?

30 hello my name is AMINEKO!

Double Take

Amineko and sushi, are they distant cousins?

They look so similar.

Line them up!

Then stack them up! They all came tumbling down!

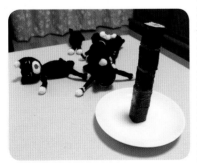

Tangerine Dreams

We only have one tangerine so it's first come, first served.

Argggggg, give me that!

Let's get some control here. There are nine of us but only eight slices.

This is mine and I'm *not* sharing!

Day Off

Where should I go today?

The sun feels so good, maybe another 10 minutes...

Hours later...
Hey, it's lunchtime!

2 p.m.: My turn for a rest.

4 p.m.: It's good to be a carefree kitty.

6 p.m.: It's dinner time, wake up!

Already? I'll get up tomorrow.

Space Invaders

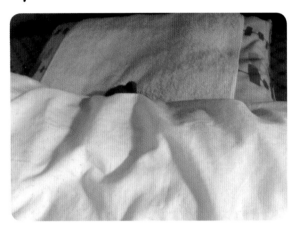

I'm so cozy.

I have the whole bed to myself.

Hey, I was here first!

This is not working at all.

Dozing Off

Too much play makes us very tired.

So tired we can sleep sitting up.

Rinnnnnng!
Ahhhh!

I saw my nine lives flash in front of my eyes!
Me too!

BEST EVER CAT NAP POSITIONS

Sacked out!

Make your own pillow.

Cozy up and stay warm.

Shield your eyes from the light.

Gaze up at the sky.

Hold onto your best friend.

And if you have a lot of best friends...

I'm not touching you! (Hee Hee) Yes you are!

Hold on to each other.

I'm still not touching you... (Hee Hee) UGH...

Four square!

CREATURE COMFORTS

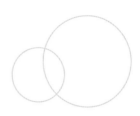

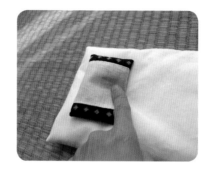

Preparing Amineko's bed is very important.

Be sure to press down on the center of the pillow.

This way they can cozy right in.

Beware, they may choose your bed instead...

...and then you'll never get them up!

Insomnia

I can't sleep, I'm so lonely.

Where's my fish? That would help.

Naughty fish! You come back to bed.

Ahhhhhhhhhh...

Fish Pillow

Lie Amineko down on the paper.

Draw an appropriate size fish.

Make a pattern from your drawing and sew a fish pillow.

Fish come in all kinds of shapes and sizes.

How about a flounder that's a bit rounder?

See pages 90 and 91 for instructions on making a fish pillow
and pages 98 and 99 for fish pillow patterns.

Napping In The Sun

There's nothing finer than soaking up the warm rays.

Is this the Reiki healing group?

White's so pale. He needs sun block!

I'm feelin' it...

I'll be your sun block!

I don't know what they're up to, but I'm just gonna take a nap.

Me too!

It always ends with a nap...

Class Photo 1

Say cheese!

Now pyramid...

Pile!

Class Photo 2

Ready, set...

...hey! What are you doing up there!

Show off...we'll show you...

Dressing Up

Aminekos rarely wear clothes, but they always wear bloomers with a dress.

And they always wear a swimsuit when going for a dip.

Fill her up!!
Ummm, that's kind of deep...maybe a little less...

Watermelon Wear

Look, I'm dressed as the rind!

I am the beautiful fruit.

You aren't the fruit, you're the slippery seeds!

I ♥ Pockets

Hmmm, there's gotta be one around here.

A-ha! And there's money inside!

I love pockets!

Snuggle Bag

I just had this bag made for me but I think it's too big. Nah, it looks great!

Fresh air and friends—there's no better way to nap!

See pages 96 and 97 for instructions on making a Snuggle bag.

Zen Kitty

Is that our new teacher?

Yes, I hear he is an enlightened spiritual master.

Close your eyes and relax your paws.

Meow-Ommmm...

Hospitality

Time to practice serving green tea and a snack. Here. Please enjoy them while they are cold.

Did I sound hospitable?

Let me move your tea over so it is easier for you. Woah! Watch out, the glass is quite slippery.

Hey, I'm not on the menu...

Picnic Blues

Blue forgot to bring the lunch.

Cheer up Blue, we can still have fun.

The best part of a picnic is being outside with friends. I'm not even hungry.

Let's play a game watching clouds!

What do you see? I see cotton catnip!

Here Comes the Sun

What are you looking at?

Now what are you looking at?

The sunrise!

The sunset!

I have to wait a whole twelve hours for the next one. (Sigh...)

AMINEKO'S BODY LANGUAGE

The Classic Sulk

Classic sulk while itching...

Forward-bend pout...

Melt down!

Watching ants...

Feeling guilty after swatting ants...

The Birds & the Bees

The Kitty Corner

This little Romeo...

If Amineko goes missing, ask yourself:

...waits for his Juliet.

Where would I go if I were a naughty kitty?

He likes to hold her soft paw.

Together they watch for birds and bees outside the window.

...a hidden, tight corner of course.

Climbing Trees

And now, for a short nature interlude. (Imagine Cat Stevens' music playing in the background of course...)

Playing Outside

Run!

Trains

Blue: "I love watching trains!"

Blue: "I wish it would hurry up and get here. Oh, here comes one!"

Blue: "The Yamanote-line! Cool!"

Blue: "Wow, that's a really long one."

Blue returned the next day for more entertainment.

Handrail Sliding

Kote: "Weeeee!"

Whump! Failed landing.

Kote: "Awesome! I was flying!"

Hanging Out

Thump!
You OK?

There's no room
for me to sit.

Let's sit over
here so we can
all fit.

Thump!

Walk!

Not again...

FELIX

Felix loves stuffing!

"Woo hoo!"

"Let's put a lot of stuffing inside."

Felix: "Awesome! I'm going in!"

A few hours later...

Blue is very happy having big brother. But...

Blue: "Wait a minute. Where did Felix go? He was playing around here a little while ago."

Blue: "Hmmm, that's strange."

Blue: "Do you know where Felix went?"

Blue: "Felix? Shhh, I think he's inside?!"

Blue: "I'm going to need you to lie down."

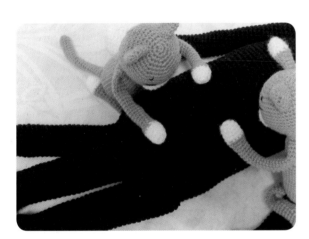

Blue: "Felix! Are you OK?!"
Green: "Can you breathe?!"

Felix: "Oh no, they know I took some of the stuffing. I'm in BIG trouble. What am I gonna do?"

Blue: "Felix! Felix Feeeeelix!"

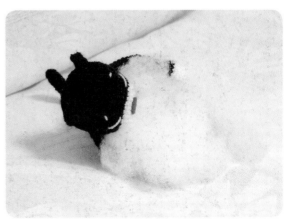

Felix: Maybe they won't see me over here...

PART 11:
HOW TO MAKE AMINEKO

WHY IS MY HOUSE FILLED WITH CROCHETED CATS?

Crafty Cats

At night when you sleep...

Blue's also getting crafty.

Amineko may be crocheting little ones.

In the morning...

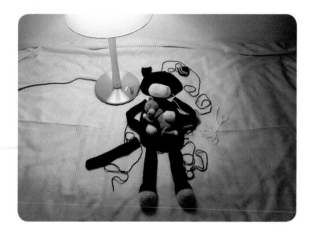

Zzzzz...

You might wake up to a larger family!

! Don't leave crochet needles laying about at night unless you want your Amineko family to grow.

Family Meeting

Is everyone here?

Someone's been crocheting at night again.

When we said big brother...

...we didn't mean literally.

Done yet?

I want a little sister.

Will someone please come and make her?

Maybe I have to do it myself.

Who am I kidding? I don't know how to crochet!

Selecting Yarn

You can use many types of yarn to achieve different looks. These beautiful Aminekos were made with specialty yarns. One is a fluffy mohair and the other a special loop yarn. They can be difficult to work with because the stitches are difficult to see, so make sure you are comfortable with the stitches and pattern before attempting to use these yarns.

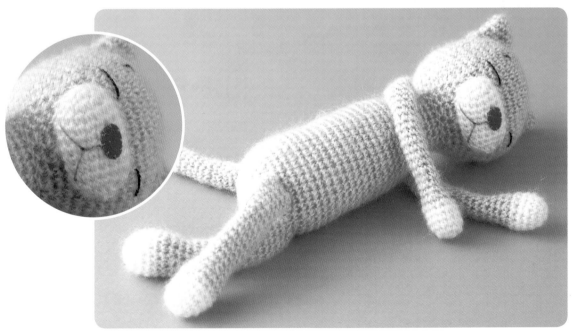

All good friends and each with their own style!

It's easy to customize your Amineko, just change the colors as you go!
You can even change their facial expressions.
Some are happy, some are sleeping and some are just chilling out.
See page 87 for the patterns.

HAVING FUN WITH YARN!

What should I make with this?

Eyeglasses?

Sunglasses?

How about bangs?

Hmm? What is this?

It's a pair of goggles!

No, a mustache!

How about crazy eyebrows?

Soba noodles on my head...what a mess.

Yarn Weight & Texture

Different weights of yarn will affect the size of your Amineko. A smooth, lightweight-yarn will result in a smaller doll and a bulky-weight, multi-fiber yarn will make a larger one. For beginners, it is best to choose a medium to thick, smooth yarn. This will make it easier to crochet and you will be able to see your stitches more clearly. Changing the size of your crochet needle will also affect the size: the smaller the needle and yarn, the smaller the Amineko.

Thick-weight yarn, 11 3/4 inches (30 cm) tall

Medium-weight yarn, 9 inches (23 cm) tall

Medium-thick-weight yarn, 10 5/8 inches (27 cm) tall

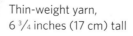

Thin-weight yarn, 6 3/4 inches (17 cm) tall

AMINEKO PATTERN

For detailed instructions, refer to pages 74 to 77 and 100 to 103.

You will use single crochet throughout. The first row of each piece will create the starting round. Begin each row by chaining two stitches then crocheting the number of stitches indicated in the "Number of Stitches" column into the first stitch, or use the yarn ring technique on page 101. Once completed, follow the directions in the "Memo" column to complete the row.

- *Increase (inc) = Add two single crochet to one stitch*
- *Decrease (dec) = Single crochet two stitches together*
- *Yarn Over Hook = YO*
- *Work Even = Single stitch entire row*

HEAD

ROW	# OF STITCHES	MEMO
1	6	make 6 sc into a ring
2	12	2 sc in each st
3	18	2 sc inc in every 2nd st
4	24	sc inc in every 3rd st
5	30	sc inc in every 4th st
6	36	sc inc in every 5th st
7	42	sc inc in every 6th st
8	48	sc inc in every 7th st
9-15	48	work even
16	42	dec in every 7th st
17	36	dec in every 6th st
18	30	dec in every 5th st
19	24	dec in every 4th st
20	18	dec in every 3rd st

ARMS (MAKE 2)
After 5 rows, change color of yarn.

ROW	# OF STITCHES	MEMO
1	6	make 6 sc into a ring
2	12	2 sc in each st
3-6*	12	work even
7	9	dec in every 3rd st
8-28	9	work even

TORSO (1 PIECE)

ROW	# OF STITCHES	MEMO
1	6	make 6 sc into a ring
2	12	2 sc in each st
3	18	sc inc in every 2nd st
4	24	sc inc in every 3rd st
5	30	sc inc in every 4th st
6	36	sc inc in every 5th st
7-23	36	work even
24	30	dec in every 5th st
25-26	30	work even
27	24	dec in every 4th st
28-29	24	work even
30	18	dec in every 3rd st
31-32	18	work even

MOUTH

ROW	# OF STITCHES	MEMO
1	7	make 7 sc into a ring
2	14	2 sc in each st
3-10	14	work even
11	4	Special dec: Insert hook into front loop only, then into the next 3 sts, YO and pull yarn through all loops on hook, repeat for next 4 st, repeat for next 3 st, repeat for next 4 st

LEGS (MAKE 2)
After 5 rows, change color of yarn.

ROW	# OF STITCHES	MEMO
1	6	make 6 sc into a ring
2	12	2 sc in each st
3	15	sc inc every 4th st
4-7*	15	work even
8	11	dec every 3rd st
9-24	11	work even

EARS (MAKE 2)

ROW	# OF STITCHES	MEMO
1	4	make 4 sc into a ring
2	8	2 sc in each st
3	10	sc inc every 4th st
4	12	sc inc every 5th st
5	14	sc inc every 6th st

TAIL (1 PIECE)

ROW	# OF STITCHES	MEMO
1	6	make 6 sc into a ring
2	8	2 sc in every 3rd st
3-22	8	work even

CONSTRUCTING YOUR AMINEKO

Begin by making the head. Once finished, crochet the torso, arms, legs, ears, and mouth pieces. The look and size of your Amineko will vary depending on the type of yarn you choose, how loose or tightly you crochet, as well as how densely you pack the filling. Aminekos come in all shapes and sizes so create the look that you like best!

Crocheting

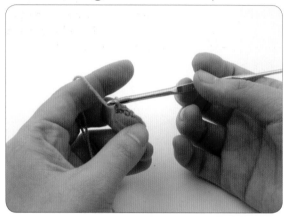

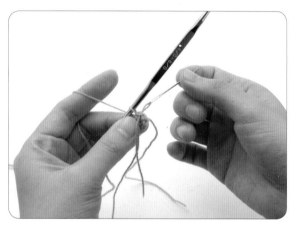

1 Crochet a foundation chain by chaining two and single crocheting the number of stitches indicated for the first round.

2 Thread a yarn needle and mark the end of the first row so you can easily locate it.

3 Increase stitches accordingly to pattern and continue crocheting.

4 Once finished increasing, begin decreasing stitches.

Stuffing

5 While making the arms, add pellets at the tip of hands.

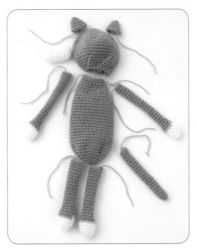

6 Your Amineko is ready to be filled!

7 Fill ⅓ of the torso with pellets and the remainder with cotton. Fill arms (hands only) and legs with pellets. Fill head and mouth with cotton. Do not fill tail.

Tips for Stuffing

Make sure body parts are solid but still soft to the touch. Your Amineko should look relaxed.

Too much stuffing: Your Amineko should have a rounded back rather than a stiff one.

Too little stuffing: If you do not use enough stuffing, it will not show the shape well.

Pinning

8 Carefully align body parts while pinning.

9 Position legs and tail so it can sit. Arms should be set a little back from the middle. Pin legs and arms to torso before stitching.

Will you please make me a friend?

Making the Face

10 Using a yarn needle, sew on ears (slightly back) and mouth.

11 Stitch on felt nose. To make mouth, eyes, and eyebrows, knot yarn or embroidery thread and insert needle in the bottom of the neck. Exit on face to stitch features. When finished, exit needle at neck and knot.

Assembly

⑫ Match the head and torso. Use a yarn needle and whip stitch stitches together one by one.

⑬ Using whip stitches attach the arms, legs, and tail.

All that's left is for you to give it a name and lots of love!

AMINEKO EXPRESSIONS

Centered Eyebrows

High set

Middle set

Low set

Far apart   Normal   Centered

Staring contest

Let's have a staring contest.

Ready, set, go!
Whoever laughs first loses!

Stay focused.

Blue: "Ha ha ha! You win!"

Wide-set Eyebrows

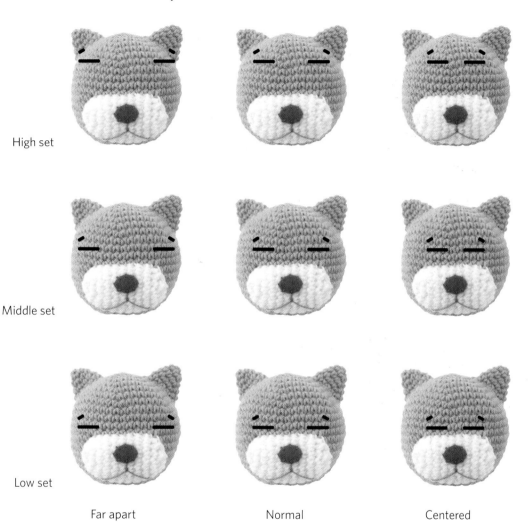

High set

Middle set

Low set

Far apart   Normal   Centered

You can vary the face of your Amineko by shifting the placement of its eyes and eyebrows.

Try different combinations to find your favorite expression.

LARGE AMINEKO PATTERN

This Amineko is twice the size of the regular one. Seated together the two sizes look like a big and little brother. The instructions are the same as for the normal size, but you will need four times the yarn and it can be crocheted more tightly. To make even larger, use thicker yarn. Mark the rows carefully because it will be difficult to count stitches. Fill with stuffing fully but due to the size, it is best to fill the arms and legs lightly with stuffing rather than pellets. This will keep them from stretching out. You will use single crochet throughout. The first row of each piece will create the starting chain. Begin each row by chaining two and single crocheting the number of stitches indicated in the "Number of Stitches" column in the first stitch. Once completed, follow the directions in the "Memo" column to complete the row.

- **Increase (inc) = Add two single crochet to one stitch**
- **Decrease (dec) = Single crochet two stitches together**
- **Yarn Over Hook = YO**
- **Work Even = Single stitch entire row**

MOUTH
For the mouth use different color yarn

	# OF STITCHES	MEMO
1	7	make 7 sc into a ring
2	14	2 sc in each st
3	21	sc inc in every 2nd st
4	28	sc inc in every 3rd st
5-19	28	work even
20	21	dec in every 3rd st
At this time fill with stuffing		
21	14	dec in every 2nd st
22	4	Special dec: Insert hook into front loop only, then into the next 3 sts, YO and pull yarn through all loops on hook, repeat for next 4 st, repeat for next 3 st, repeat for next 4 st

HEAD

	# OF STITCHES	MEMO
1	6	make 6 sc into a ring
2	12	2 sc in each st
3	18	sc inc in every 2nd st
4	24	sc inc in every 3rd st
5	30	sc inc in every 4th st
6	36	sc inc in every 5th st
7	42	sc inc in every 6th st
8	48	sc inc in every 7th st
9	54	sc inc in every 8th st
10	60	sc inc in every 9th st
11	66	sc inc in every 10th
12	72	sc inc in 11th st
13	78	sc inc in every 12th st
14	84	sc inc in every 13th st
15	90	sc inc in every 14th st
16	96	sc inc in every 15th st
17-30	96	work even
31	90	dec in every 15th st
32	84	dec in every 14th st
33	78	dec in every 13th st
34	72	dec in every 12th st
35	66	dec in every 11th st
36	60	dec in every 10th st
37	54	dec in every 9th st
38	48	dec in every 8th st
39	42	dec in every 7th st
40	36	dec in every 6th st

TORSO

	# OF STITCHES	MEMO
1	6	make 6 sc into a ring
2	12	2 sc in each st
3	18	sc inc in every 2nd st
4	24	sc inc in every 3rd st
5	30	sc inc in every 4th st
6	36	sc inc in every 5th st
7	42	sc inc in every 6th st
8	48	sc inc in every 7th st
9	54	sc inc in every 8th st
10	60	sc inc in every 9th st
11	66	sc inc in every 10th
12	72	sc inc in every 11th st
13-46	72	work even
47	66	dec in every 11th st
48-49	66	work even
50	60	dec in every 10th st
51-52	60	work even
53	54	dec in every 9th st
54-55	54	work even
56	48	dec in every 8th st
57-58	48	work even
59	42	dec in every 7th st
60-61	42	work even
62	36	dec in every 6th st
63-64	36	work even

EARS (MAKE 2)
*For a striped ear make rows 7 and 9 in a different color

	# OF STITCHES	MEMO
1	4	make 4 sc into a ring
2	8	8 sc in each st
3	12	sc inc in every 2nd st
4	16	sc inc in every 3rd st
5	18	sc inc in every 8th st
6	20	sc inc in every 9th st
7*	22	sc inc in every 10th st
8	24	sc inc in every 11th st
9*	26	sc inc in every 12th st
10	28	sc inc in every 13th st

LEGS (MAKE 2)
*Change color of yarn at 10th row

	# OF STITCHES	MEMO
1	6	make 6 sc into a ring
2	12	2 sc in each st
3	18	sc inc in every 2nd st
4	24	sc inc in every 3rd st
5	27	sc inc in every 8th st
6	30	sc inc in every 9th st
7-15*	30	work even
16	20	dec in every 2nd st
17-48	20	work even

ARMS (MAKE 2)
*Change color of yarn at 10th row

	# OF STITCHES	MEMO
1	6	make 6 sc into a ring
2	12	2 sc in each st
3	18	sc inc in every 2nd st
4	24	sc inc in every 3rd st
5-13*	24	work even
14	16	dec in every 2nd st
15-56	16	work even

TAIL

	# OF STITCHES	MEMO
1	6	make 6 sc into a ring
2	12	2 sc in each st
3	16	sc inc in every 3rd st
4-44	16	work even

Big Brother Little Brother

A medium-weight yarn was used to make the large Amineko pattern. A thin yarn was used with the standard-size pattern.

PREPARE YOUR MATERIALS

Yarn

Choose your favorite color and texture. For beginners, it is best to begin with a medium-weight, straight yarn instead of a specialty yarn.

CROCHET NEEDLE, YARN NEEDLE, PIN, EMBROIDERY NEEDLE
The needle size noted on yarn packaging is only a suggestion. Each person's preference for what feels comfortable will vary so try different sizes to learn what suits you best. I tend to crochet very tightly, so I use a #6 needle with medium thick yarn.

TYPES OF PELLETS
Pellets (available at most sewing and craft stores) are used to give weight to the Amineko's bottom and the tips of the arms and legs. If small children will be playing with your Amineko, be sure the pellets won't squeeze out from between the stitches. They are very dangerous for children to swallow. To keep the pellets contained, fill pantyhose with them before stuffing. You may also use small rocks, toy bullets, or marbles.

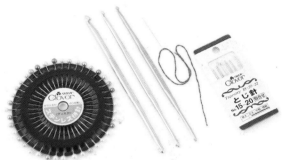

Alternatives for pellets (left to right) ball bearings, marbles, rocks, toy bullets

How to Make Amineko **85**

Making Clothing and Accessories

FABRICS
Use to make futons, zabuton pillow, and clothes.

EMBROIDERY THREAD
Use for eyes, eyebrows, and mouth. For a less shiny look, use a thin yarn.

FABRIC COLOR AND PENS
Use to decorate fabric.

STUFFING
Use to fill your Amineko.

FELT
Use to make the nose. It can also be used for eyes or a tongue.

DESIGN YOUR OWN!

It's easy to customize your Amineko by simply changing colors while crocheting. Below are different patterns to get you started. The numbers on the pattern indicate the approximate row numbers where you will need to change colors.

AMINEKO ACCESSORIES

Don't you want your Amineko to be cozy and comfortable? Stitch them up
a futon or a zabuton meditation pillow and they will love you forever!

Futon Mattress

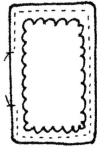

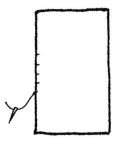

❶ Place two fabric squares
together (wrong sides out) and
stitch edges. Leave opening so
it can be turned right side out.

❷ Turn right side out, add stuffing
evenly, and stitch closed.

Futon Cover—Repeat steps above.

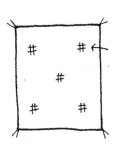

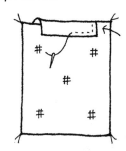

To hold stuffing in place, tack
layers together with stitches as
illustrated with # marks.

Stitch on white fabric
at top edge.

Pillow

1 Place two fabric squares together (wrong sides out) and stitch edges. Leave opening so it can be turned right side out.

2 Fill with pellets and stitch closed.

3 Use white fabric to make pillowcase, if desired.

Zabuton Meditation Pillow

1 Place two fabric squares together (wrong sides out) and stitch edges. Leave opening so it can be turned right side out.

2 Add stuffing evenly.

3 Stitch opening closed.

4 Add threads at each corner and one in the center.

Single knot and cut thread

 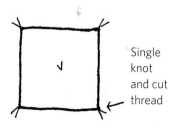

FISH PILLOW

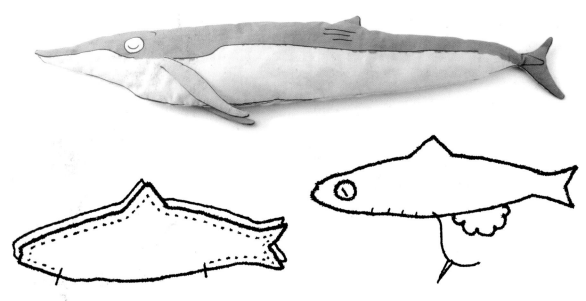

1 Using the pattern on page 99, cut the fabric along the pattern line (wrong side out). Stitch edges together leaving an opening so it can be turned right side out.

2 Turn right side out, fill with stuffing, and stitch closed.

For the goldfish, it will be easy to turn inside out if you leave this section open.

(Goldfish pattern on p. 99)

DRIED CUTTLEFISH PILLOW

1 Using the pattern on page 98, cut the fabric along the pattern line (wrong side out). Stitch edges together leaving an opening so it can be turned right side out.

2 Sew here and fill lightly with stuffing

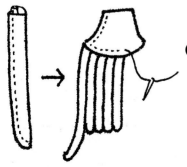

3 Sew long, thin strips of fabrics together to make 10 tentacles. Stitch together onto their base.

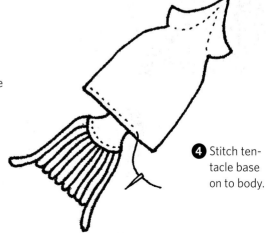

4 Stitch tentacle base on to body.

Kitty Clothes

For actual size, enlarge pattern 200% and add $1/4$ inch (6 cm) seam allowances.

Watermelon Dress

The back left panel should be slightly wider than the right to accommodate snap closure. Use adhesive interfacing to finish edges around neck and sleeves.

(Enlarge pattern 200%)

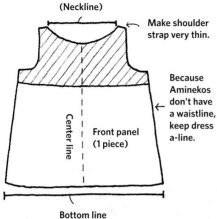

(Neckline)

Make shoulder strap very thin.

Because Aminekos don't have a waistline, keep dress a-line.

Center line

Front panel (1 piece)

Bottom line
(Measure thickest part of waist and add a little extra. Half of that = correct width.)

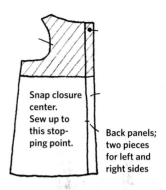

Snap closure center. Sew up to this stopping point.

Back panels; two pieces for left and right sides

Add adhesive interfacing

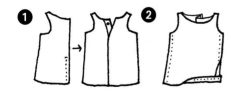

❶ Place back panels together (wrong sides out) and stitch up the center to the stopping point. Attach snap closure.

❷ Place front and back panels together (wrong sides out) and stitch the sides and shoulders. Hem bottom edge and turn right side out.

Speedy Swim Trunks

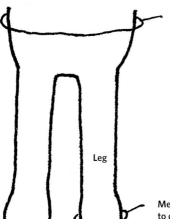

The circumference of the suit's waist should be slightly larger than your Amineko's waist.

Leg

Measure thickest part of the leg to determine circumference of leg openings.

1. Cut fabric for front panels and leave extra room for snap. Stitch front panels together.

2. Stitch top back panels together.

3. Stitch bottom back panels together.

4. Stitch top back and bottom back panels together. Opening for tail should be in the center.

5. Stitch front panels (2 pieces) to back panels (4 pieces). Follow letter indications on pattern matching the As, Bs, and Cs together. Apply snap closure and finish seam allowance. Stitch stripes with embroidery thread.

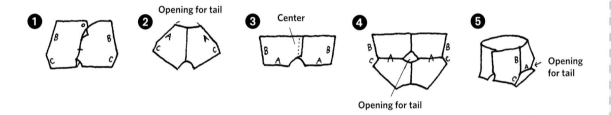

Pattern of swimming suit
Enlarge 200%

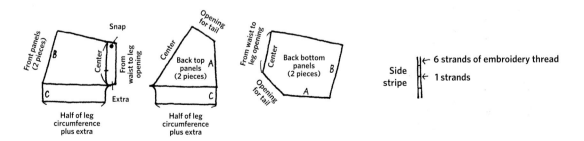

Snuggle Bag

Measure your Amineko for a perfectly sized snuggle bag.

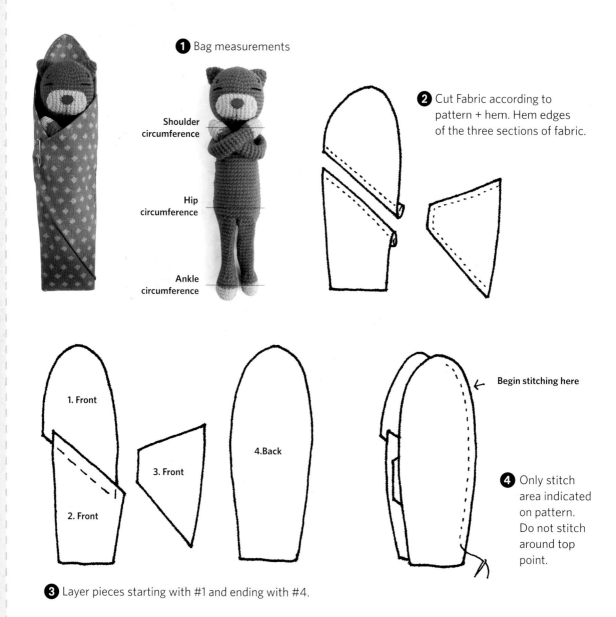

1 Bag measurements

Shoulder circumference

Hip circumference

Ankle circumference

2 Cut Fabric according to pattern + hem. Hem edges of the three sections of fabric.

1. Front

2. Front

3. Front

4. Back

Begin stitching here

4 Only stitch area indicated on pattern. Do not stitch around top point.

3 Layer pieces starting with #1 and ending with #4.

5 Turn right side out and apply snap or ribbon closure of your choice. A safety pin is the easiest.

Look how cute your Amineko is! →

Snuggle Bag Pattern
(enlarge approx. 200%)

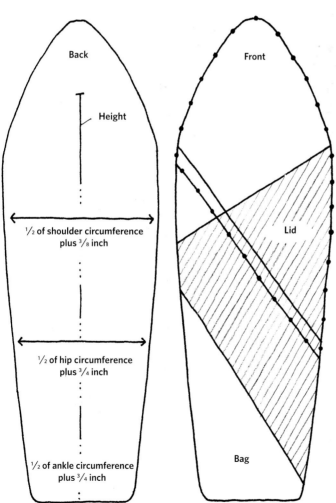

Back

Height

½ of shoulder circumference plus ⅜ inch

½ of hip circumference plus ¾ inch

½ of ankle circumference plus ¾ inch

Front

Lid

Bag

Back
Front
Bag
Lid

} 1 each

FISH PILLOW PATTERNS

Small Fish Pillow
Enlarge 200%

Dried Cuttlefish Pillow
Enlarge 200%

Flatfish Pillow
Enlarge 200%

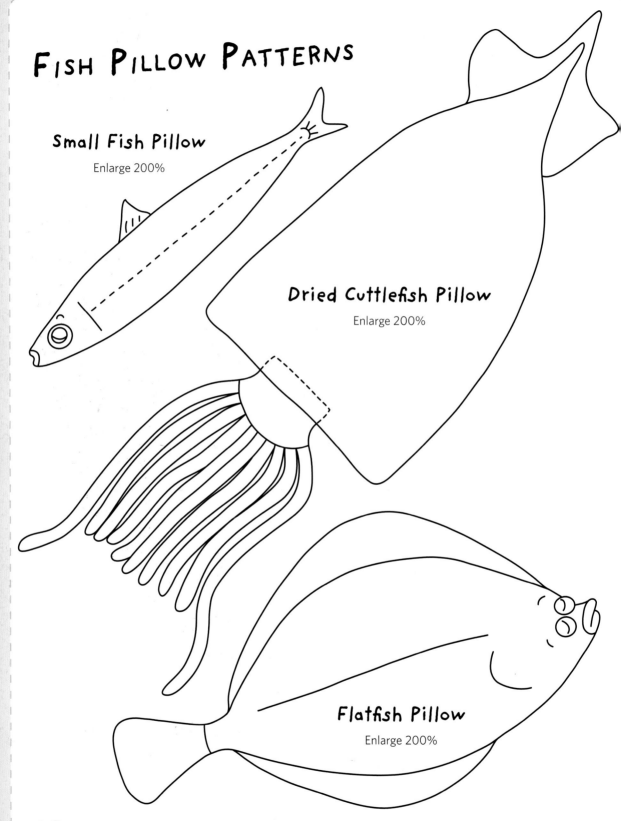

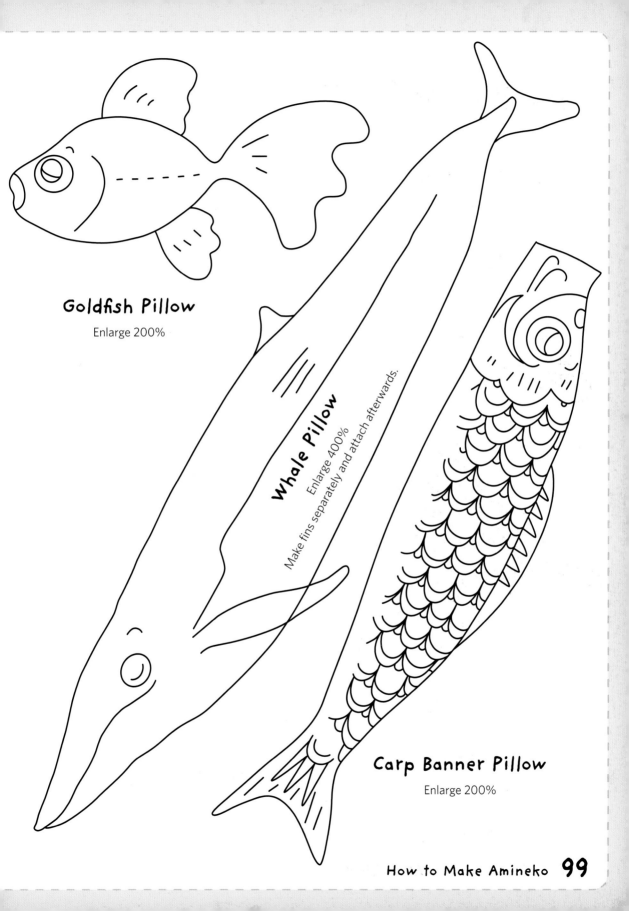

Goldfish Pillow

Enlarge 200%

Whale Pillow

Enlarge 400%

Make fins separately and attach afterwards.

Carp Banner Pillow

Enlarge 200%

Basic Crocheting

These basic crochet instructions are all you need to make your Amineko.
Once you get the hang of them, it goes very quickly. Have fun!

How to hold the yarn and crochet hook

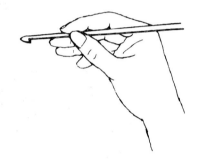

- **Crochet hook** (right hand)
  Facing the hook down, place it between your thumb and index finger. Use middle finger for support.
- **Yarn** (left hand)

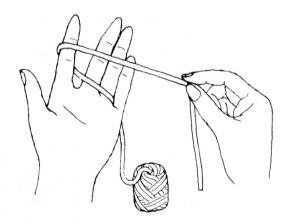

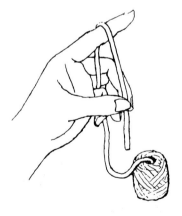

1 Lace yarn between your pinky and fourth finger. Bring yarn across palm and behind index finger. Wrap yarn back around to cross fingers.

2 Holding end of yarn between thumb and middle finger, loop yarn over your straightened index finger to control tension.

Single crochet (starting from a yarn ring)

1 Hold end of yarn with thumb and middle finger and wrap twice around index finger.

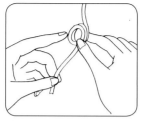

2 Remove ring with right hand.

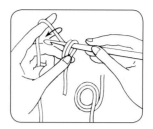

3 Shift ring to left hand and bring yarn over left index finger. Insert hook in ring, hook yarn and pull back through ring.

4 To make one chain stitch, wrap yarn over hook and pull through previous loop on hook as arrow indicates.

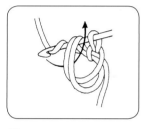

5 Next, do a single stitch. Insert hook into ring, wrap yarn over hook, and pull back out.

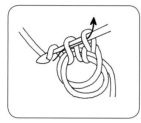

6 Wrap yarn over hook again and pull through two previous loops.

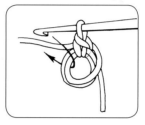

7 Repeat steps 5 and 6 until the required number of single stitches have been made.

8 When finished, remove hook and pull yarn from inside of ring.

9 Pull end of yarn to tighten ring.

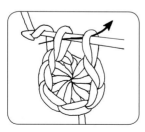

10 To finish first row, insert hook, wrap yarn over hook, and pull through two loops to make single stitch.

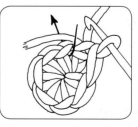

11 While crocheting second row, hide edge of yarn.

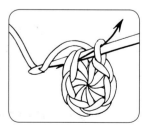

12 At end of row, insert hook in the first stitch and pull yarn back through.

More Crochet Basics

- Single crochet once over two stitches (decreases one stitch)

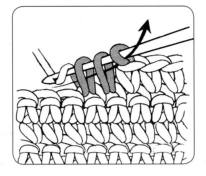 

- Two single crochet in single stitch (increases one stitch)

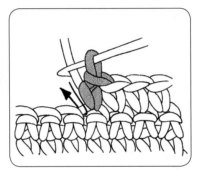 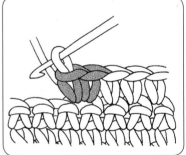

- Insert hook in stitch, yarn over and pull through (Slip stitch)

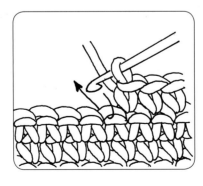 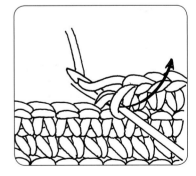

hello my name is AMINEKO!

IMPORTANT TECHNIQUES

• **A standing point will make a clean line when changing color.**

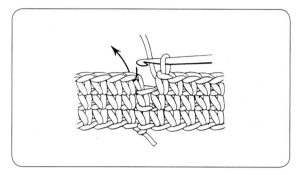

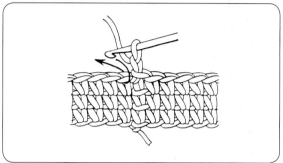

❶ At end of row insert hook at first stitch, wrap yarn over hook, and pull out.

❷ Make one chain stitch, insert hook to the same stitch, and make a single stitch.

• **Changing color of yarn**

• **Seaming (twist stitch)**

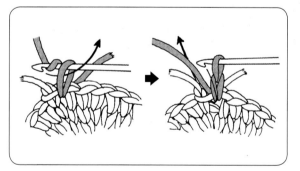

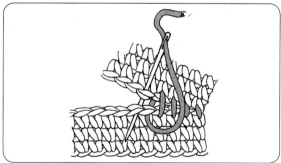

At the required row, slip stitch and then cut yarn. Insert hook into the same stitch, pull the new yarn through and make a chain stitch. Make single stitch at the same place.

Align crocheted pieces and stitch under both threads of every single stitch with yarn needle.

hello my name is AMINEKO!